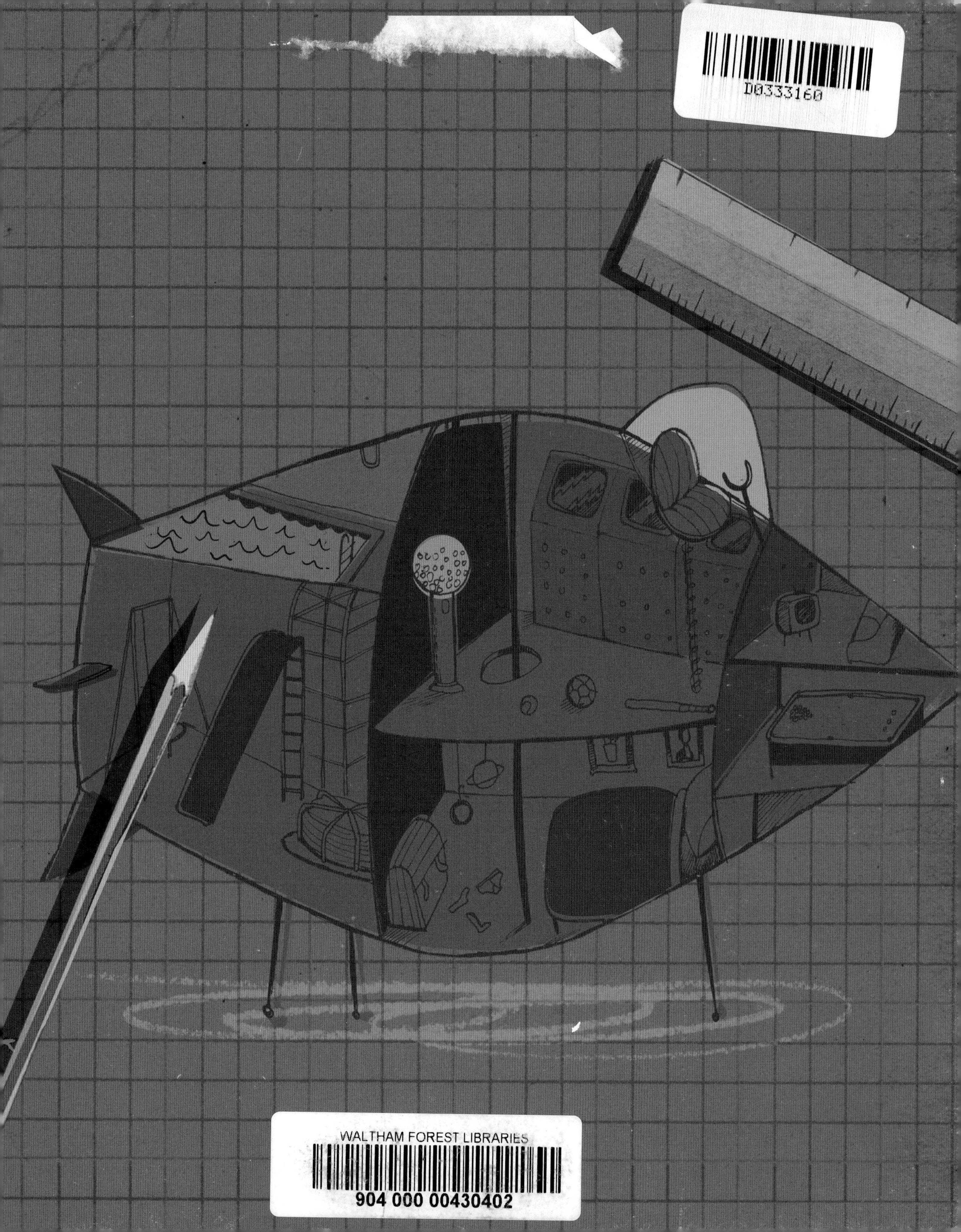

Great Clarendon Street, Oxford OX2 6DP

Oxford University Press is a department of the
University of Oxford. It furthers the University's
objective of excellence in research, scholarship, and
education by publishing worldwide in

Oxford New York

Auckland Cape Town Dar es Salaam Hong Kong Karachi
Kuala Lumpur Madrid Melbourne Mexico City Nairobi
New Delhi Shanghai Taipei Toronto

With offices in

Argentina Austria Brazil Chile Czech Republic France Greece
Guatemala Hungary Italy Japan Poland Portugal Singapore
South Korea Switzerland Thailand Turkey Ukraine Vietnam

Oxford is a registered trade mark of Oxford University Press
in the UK and in certain other countries

This book first published 2015

2 4 6 8 10 9 7 5 3 1

British Library Cataloguing in Publication Data

Data available

ISBN: 978-0-19-273633-8 (hardback)
ISBN: 978-0-19-273634-5 (paperback)

Printed in China

Paper used in the production of this book is a natural,
clable product made from wood grown in sustainable forests.

For Ben, the alien
who rocks
my world – S.P-H. x

To Dad,
much love –
T.M.

To find out more about Smriti's
books go to: www.smriti.co.uk

My Alien and Me

Smriti Prasadam-Halls
and Tom McLaughlin

OXFORD
UNIVERSITY PRESS

Guess what!

I've found a real live ALIEN!

Here he is!

He's all the way from
planet Earth.
Imagine that!

That is his spaceship.
Oops!

Luckily, my Dad is a UFO expert so he can fix it. Till then, the alien is staying with me!

Mum said my alien had better have a wash and a spot of breakfast after his long journey . . .

but I don't think he likes slime baths . . .

or Jupiter jellyfish.

When we got to school, he REALLY didn't like the look of my teacher, Miss Eight-Eyes.

It was quite embarrassing at lunch time because my alien REFUSED to eat with his toes!

And after school, when I took him to the playground, he couldn't moonwalk OR solar surf.

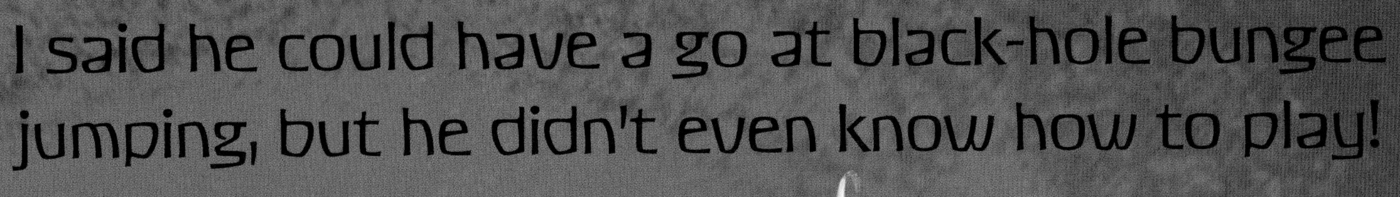
I said he could have a go at black-hole bungee jumping, but he didn't even know how to play!

I don't want to look after my alien anymore.

My alien LOOKS strange.
He ACTS strange.

And he doesn't
know how to
play ANY
good games . . .

'I wish you'd go home!'
I said.

A little tear
rolled down my
alien's cheek.

That night it was strange because I just couldn't get to sleep. I had such a sad feeling in my tummy.

I wanted to talk to my alien, but he **was gone!**

I checked
the
Crater Café . . .

and the
Lunar
Lighthouse . . .

and the
Asteroid Adventure
Playground, but
he wasn't
anywhere.

At last I spotted a
light in his spaceship . . .
Poor alien. I expect he's
wishing he could go home.

I went up to the door. I think my alien could tell I was sorry. He invited me into his UFO . . .

and it was
AMAZING!

Since then I've been learning lots of things about my alien and his planet.

He's taught me about funny aliens called **pirates** . . .

and ferocious aliens called **dinosaurs.**

He's even shown me how to play alien rock guitar!

My alien is enjoying some of our ways, too.

And he's become a solar surfing champion!

In fact, I'm not sure that aliens are really all that different from us after all.

They're just a bit uglier.

And some of us don't seem to think they're ugly at all.

We've been having lots of fun, my alien and me, but today Dad told us that the spaceship is fixed.

I don't want my alien to leave, but he has to go . . . He's got a mum and dad, too. He's even got an annoying little sister, like I do!

'I'll miss you,' I say as my alien
boards his spaceship.

And then I realise . . .
MY ALIEN isn't MY alien at all.
He's . . .

my FRIEND.

My friend has
made me promise
to write to him,
but I'm going to
do much better
than that . . .

I'm planning a surprise visit!
I hope all the other aliens will be
pleased to see me!